✚ Doll Hospital ✚

Glory's Freedom
A STORY OF
THE UNDERGROUND RAILROAD

Doll Hospital #1
Tatiana Comes to America
AN ELLIS ISLAND STORY

Doll Hospital #2
Goldie's Fortune
A STORY OF
THE GREAT DEPRESSION

Doll Hospital #3
Glory's Freedom
A STORY OF
THE UNDERGROUND RAILROAD

Coming Soon

Doll Hospital #4
Charlotte's Choice
THE STORY OF
A SHAKER VILLAGE

✚ Doll Hospital ✚

Glory's Freedom

A STORY OF
THE UNDERGROUND RAILROAD

BY JOAN HOLUB

Illustrations by Cheryl Kirk Noll

A LITTLE APPLE PAPERBACK

SCHOLASTIC INC.

New York   Toronto   London   Auckland   Sydney
Mexico City   New Delhi   Hong Kong   Buenos Aires

ISBN 0-439-40180-1

Design by Steve Scott

12 11 10 9 8 7 6 5 4 3 2 1   3 4 5 6 7 8/0

Printed in the U.S.A.   40
First Scholastic printing, January 2003

For Joy Peskin, who thought of doll hospitals.

*With thanks to my mom for taking me and
my doll Annie to a doll hospital.*

—*J.H.*

Table of Contents

✚ Doll Hospital ✚

Glory's Freedom
A STORY OF
THE UNDERGROUND RAILROAD

CHAPTER 1
❖ Doll Auction ❖

Wow! Look at all these dolls!" said Rose.

Rose, Lila, and their grandmother walked underneath a big banner inside the Oak Hill Convention Center. Lila read it aloud: "WINTER DOLL AUCTION. HUNDREDS OF ANTIQUE DOLLS FOR SHOW AND SALE."

Everywhere they looked there were long tables with dolls on them. Some of the dolls were on shelves or inside glass cases. Guards stood nearby.

"Are all these dolls for sale?" asked Rose.

"Most of them," said Far Nana. "They'll be sold in the auction later this morning."

Far Nana was the nickname they'd given their grandmother five years ago, when Rose was five and Lila was three. It was because she lived far away from their apartment back in the city. Near Nana was their other grandmother. She lived close by.

Rose and Lila were living with Far Nana for a year while their parents were in Africa. Their mom and dad were doctors who specialized in treating rare diseases. The African villages where they were working weren't safe enough for Rose and Lila. So the girls had to stay behind in America at Far Nana's. They couldn't stay with Near Nana because the building she lived in was only for older people.

"We have an hour to view the dolls before the auction starts," Far Nana told Rose and Lila. "I'll check in at the registration desk and get a bidding card. You girls can go look around."

"What's over there?" Lila pointed at some smaller rooms nearby. One had a sign that said: DOLL BODY SHOP.

"Those are stores with doll-related items for sale," said Far Nana. "Things like doll clothes that won't be in the auction."

"Let's go see the dolls before we look in there," Rose told Lila.

"No! Let's go in those shops first." Lila hurried off before Rose could stop her.

Inside the Doll Body Shop, there were more long tables with boxes on top. Three grown-ups stood talking at one end of the shop. Rose and Lila went to the opposite end to look around.

Rose peeked into one of the boxes. It was full of loose doll legs and feet.

Lila pulled out a big pinkish arm and a small brown

arm. "Look!" she said. "You can buy doll arms for just fifty cents. Want to?"

"What would we do with a bunch of arms?" asked Rose. "Make an arm-y?"

"I don't know," said Lila. "But I don't have enough money to buy a whole doll. I want to buy something."

"Let's keep looking," said Rose.

Lila pulled a small fashion doll head with long blond hair from one box and showed it to Rose. "This one looks like you."

Rose nodded. She was digging around in a box full of mismatched doll parts. "You know, you could make a weird doll out of this stuff."

Lila lay the fashion doll head on the table and put a big baby-doll body under it. Then she added two different kinds of arms, one short leg, and one long leg.

Rose laughed at Lila's creation. "Don't become a doll maker when you grow up, Dr. Frankenstein. Promise me."

Lila grinned. "I promise nothing."

Rose pulled a green clown wig from a box and plopped it on top of her hair. She wobbled her head and made a silly face. "Look! I'm wigging out!"

"May I help you?" a grown-up voice asked from nearby.

Rose jumped in surprise, knocking over a box of doll hands. They went flying. The lady who had spoken frowned at her.

No fair, thought Rose. She felt herself starting to blush. Lila always got away with doing all kinds of weird stuff. But the minute Rose did anything weird, somebody always saw.

The lady kneeled down and started gathering doll hands from the floor.

Rose put the green wig away and squatted down to help. "Here, let me give you a hand," she said.

The lady didn't laugh.

After they finished picking up the scattered hands, the lady pointed at the goofy doll Lila had made on the table. "That's some doll you've assembled. Maybe your mommy would like to see it. Where is your mommy, anyway?"

"Africa," said Lila.

While the lady was trying to figure that one out, Rose decided to make an escape. She gave the lady a fake smile, grabbed Lila's hand, and pulled her out the door.

They went into the next room. "Let's see what's in here," said Rose.

"Oooh! Dollhouses!" squealed Lila. She went closer to an old-fashioned dollhouse. One side was open, so they could see into the rooms full of doll-sized furniture. The five-story dollhouse was almost as tall as Lila. But Rose had to stoop to look inside.

Lila picked up a small doll with short brown hair from one of the dollhouse bedrooms.

"That doll looks like you," said Rose.

"Yeah," said Lila. "I don't have enough money for a big doll, but maybe I can buy this one."

A man who worked there walked toward them.

Lila showed him the little doll. "How much is this?"

"Twenty-two," said the man.

"Dollars?" squeaked Lila.

The man smiled. "That's right. They don't call them DOLL-ars for nothing."

Disappointed, Lila set the doll back on its chair. "Everything costs more money than I have."

"How much do you have?" asked Rose.

"Fifty-three." Lila jiggled her hand in her jeans pocket so her money clinked together. "Pennies."

Far Nana came in the shop, looking for them.

"There you are. Come along, girls. Let's go look at the dolls before the sale starts."

CHAPTER 2
❖ Doll Doctor ❖

"How much is that one?" asked Lila. She pointed at a shiny china doll in a white lace dress sitting on one of the tables in the showroom.

Rose checked the price. "Three thousand dollars!"

"No way!" said Lila.

"The doll may sell for even more than that," Far Nana told them. "That's just its starting price for the auction."

"Wow!" said Lila.

They looked around at other dolls on display. Rose and Lila picked out the dolls that cost the most. Then they picked out the weirdest ones. Then they picked out the ones they liked best.

Far Nana pulled a little flashlight from her purse.

"What's that for?" asked Rose.

"You'll see," said Far Nana.

She pointed at a pretty doll on a display table and asked the nearby guard, "Do you mind if I inspect this one?"

"It's okay to touch the dolls in this area," the guard replied.

"Thanks." Far Nana picked up the old bisque doll. She lifted its wig and shined her flashlight inside its head.

"What are you looking for? Brains?" asked Lila.

"The auction company just sells the dolls. It doesn't inspect them. Some dolls have wood rot, termites, and other types of damage," said Far Nana. "It's up to us to see what the dolls might be hiding."

"Aha! See this?" she said.

Rose and Lila leaned closer.

"There's a crack!" said Rose.

When the flashlight was on, you could see a long crack in the doll's face. When it was off, you couldn't.

"This doll has been repaired. Good job, too. I couldn't have done it better myself." Far Nana set the doll back down.

Far Nana was a doll doctor, so she knew all about dolls. She had a doll hospital in her house. People brought old or broken dolls to her, and she always knew how to fix them. Just like Rose and Lila's parents were doctors who could fix people in a people hospital.

A brown-skinned woman with black beaded braids and a camera around her neck was standing next to them. She had been watching Far Nana inspect the old bisque doll.

"Do you repair dolls?" she asked.

Far Nana nodded. "Yes, I run a doll hospital."

"My name is Andrea Tate," the woman told them. She reached out and shook hands with Far Nana. "Last week, my husband and I found an old doll in our basement. I'm taking it to the auctioneer now for today's sale."

Ms. Tate set the box she was holding on a table, opened it, and pulled out a doll.

When Far Nana saw it, she put a hand over her heart. "Oh! It's lovely!"

Rose and Lila gave each other sideways looks. The doll's black hair was tangled, and its poofy flowered skirt was stained and torn. The ribbon ties on its straw bonnet were frayed. Very tiny cracks covered its arms and legs.

Worst of all, its nose was missing!

But as usual, thought Rose, Far Nana saw beyond what a doll looked like on the outside. She could see way down to its beauty underneath.

"It looks sort of like a candle," said Rose.

"Or like Far Nana's beauty soap," said Lila.

Ms. Tate held her doll away from Rose and Lila like she didn't want them to touch it. "It's made of wax. Very delicate," she warned.

"Hint, hint," Rose whispered to Lila. "She means she doesn't want kids like us anywhere near her doll."

"As if we would hurt it!" Lila whispered back.

"The auctioneer suggested that I have the doll repaired before I tried to sell it," said Ms. Tate. "Since I didn't know of any doll hospitals, I decided to put it in the auction today as it is. If it doesn't sell, are you interested in restoring it?"

"I'd love to work on such a beautiful doll," said Far Nana. "What's its finding story?"

"Finding story? I don't understand," said Ms. Tate.

"That's what we doll people call the story of how you found the doll or where it came from."

"Oh!" Ms. Tate's voice got excited. "I'm a photographer and I'm having the basement of my house remodeled to become my office. When the construction crew began work, we found this doll hidden in the wall. I have no idea how long the doll had been there or how it got there. Too bad it can't tell us."

Rose and Lila looked at each other. Yeah, too bad, they said in silent-sister brain-wave talk.

CHAPTER 3
✦ Auction Time ✦

The auction's beginning," said Far Nana.

They said good-bye to Ms. Tate and hurried into the auction room nearby. Rose and Lila followed Far Nana to the back of the big room full of chairs. They sat down, with Far Nana in the middle.

"Why are we sitting so far back? All those seats up front are empty," said Rose.

"From back here, we'll be able to see who's bidding without turning around," explained Far Nana.

"What's bidding?" asked Lila.

Far Nana pointed toward a man wearing plaid pants, who was standing on the stage at the front of the room. "That's the auctioneer. He'll show us different dolls, one by one. He'll say a price. People in the audience can hold up their bidding cards if they want to buy the doll for that price. That's called bidding."

Once the room had filled with people, the auctioneer banged a wooden hammer on the stage podium. Everyone got quiet.

11

"Welcome-Welcome-Welcome," he boomed. "Welcome-to-the-Winter-Doll-Auction!"

"He talks faster than anybody I've ever heard!" Lila whispered.

"That's to get everyone excited about the dolls," Far Nana whispered.

"All-sales-final. Don't buy a doll if you haven't first smelled it, felt it, and held it to be sure you want it," said the auctioneer.

A helper in a red coat handed the auctioneer a doll wearing a colorful skirt. It was holding a bunch of little pots and pans.

The auctioneer showed it to the crowd. "Let's start with this peddlar doll from the late 1700s," he boomed. "Made of gen-yoo-ine treewood."

"What's treewood?" asked Rose. "Doesn't all wood come from trees?"

"That was a little auctioneer joke," said Far Nana. They spoke quietly, so they wouldn't bother anyone.

"Bidding opens at twelve hundred dollars. Where's the pleasure?" called the auctioneer.

"That means people can start bidding now," said Far Nana.

A woman sitting in front of them raised her bidding card. It had the number eighty-five on it. Other people held their numbered cards up, too.

"A crowd of bids at twelve. Do I hear thirteen fifty?" asked the auctioneer.

Only four people raised their cards this time. The price kept going up as people bid back and forth. Everyone was excited, waiting to see who would win the doll.

Seconds later, only one person was holding up a card.

"Sold to number eighty-five for eighteen hundred dollars," said the auctioneer. "Next lot."

One of the red-coated helpers handed the auctioneer another doll.

The auctioneer started again. "What am I bid for —"

"Hey, look. It's Ms. Tate's no-nose doll," said Rose.

"Do I hear one hundred fifty dollars?" asked the auctioneer.

Nobody bid.

The price went lower. And lower.

"Poor no-nose. No one wants her," said Lila.

"She needs too much work," said Far Nana.

"I feel sorry for her. Why don't you buy her?" Rose asked Far Nana.

"I'd like to buy all the dolls here, but I don't have that much money," said Far Nana.

Finally, the auctioneer said, "I'll take a bid of two quarters."

Still, nobody bid.

"Fair warning," boomed the auctioneer.

Suddenly, Lila grabbed the bidding card from Far Nana's lap and held it up. "Fifty-three cents!" she shouted.

The auctioneer smiled. "Fifty-three cents? Did you plan to buy the doll or rent it?"

"Uh . . ." said Lila. She looked at Far Nana. "What does he mean?"

Before Far Nana could answer, the auctioneer said, "Sorry, little lady. Can't sell a doll for that. House rules."

He handed the no-nose wax doll to one of his helpers to take away. "Toss her in the swamp," he told the man.

Rose and Lila gasped.

"Calm down. He's not really going to toss her in a swamp," said Far Nana. "He just means 'put the doll away'."

"But why didn't I get the doll? I bid more than two quarters," said Lila.

"I'm sorry, honey," said Far Nana. "Two quarters means fifty dollars at an auction, not fifty cents. And if he doesn't get a bid that he thinks is high enough, the auctioneer won't sell the doll to anyone."

"Oh," said Lila.

Next, the auctioneer held up a different doll. Rose, Lila, and Far Nana watched more dolls get sold. After a while, Far Nana said, "Let's go home and have lunch."

On their way out, Ms. Tate stopped them. Because

the no-nose wax doll hadn't sold, Ms. Tate wanted Far Nana to take it home and fix it in her doll hospital. While she and Far Nana talked about the doll, Lila pulled Rose toward the gift shop.

"C'mon. This is my last chance to buy something," Lila said.

Inside the shop, Lila found lots of things she wanted. But they were all too expensive.

Then she saw an ink pen with a little doll eraser-head on the end. "How much for this?" she asked the woman behind the counter.

"Fifty cents. Plus tax," the woman told her.

Lila dug in her pocket, then put her money on the counter. "Sold!"

Lila showed Rose her new pen. "Look what I got for my fifty-three pennies."

"Cute," said Rose. "I guess they don't call them PEN-nies for nothing."

CHAPTER 4
❧ Home Again ❧

When they got home, Far Nana made grilled cheese sandwiches and tomato soup. After lunch, they all went upstairs to a turreted room on the third floor where Far Nana had her doll hospital. The room was nicknamed "the witch's hat" because of its tall, pointed roof. From outside, it looked just like a witch's hat.

Inside the doll hospital, colorful spools of thread, fabric, and ribbons sat on shelves and hung out of drawers. There were boxes and bags of doll parts and accessories like eyeballs, shoes, and wigs. There were lots of dolls, too: big dolls, little dolls, and in-between size dolls.

"First of all, I have to give Ms. Tate's doll a checkup and see how much repair is needed," Far Nana told Rose and Lila. She began undressing the no-nose doll.

Lila peeked under its skirt. "I thought petticoats were making no-nose's skirt poof out so much. But it's this wooden birdcage thing."

"It's called a cage crinoline or a hoop skirt," said Far Nana. "It was fashionable for women to wear them instead of petticoats during the mid-1800s. That's a good clue that this doll was made around the time of the Civil War."

She removed the doll's hat and shoes. Then, off came the dress, hoopskirt, corset, slip, and pantaloons.

"Girls sure wore a lot of clothes back in the old days," said Rose. "We'd be late for school if we had to put all this on every morning."

"A poofy hoop skirt wouldn't fit under my desk, either," said Lila.

Far Nana studied the doll and its clothes. "This cloth body is in good shape. It won't even need washing. But these clothes will. The shoes are okay. The hat needs restitching. At least none of its straw is missing."

"Where are you going to get a new doll nose, though?" asked Rose.

Far Nana opened a cabinet and pulled out a square block of wax. "I'm going to make one out of this."

"But it's the wrong color," said Lila. "It's yellow and no-nose is more pink."

"I'll melt it and add color until it matches," said Far Nana.

"That sounds hard," said Rose.

"It is," said Far Nana. "Wax is a tricky material to repair. And to clean. Turpentine would clean it, but that might remove the doll's lip and cheek color. I'm going to try alcohol instead."

Far Nana dipped a cotton swab into rubbing alcohol and scrubbed it gently on the back of the no-nose doll's neck. A lot of dirt came off.

"Yuck! It's dirtier than it looks," said Rose.

"Wax attracts dust, so I'm not surprised," said Far Nana.

"How did you learn to fix wax dolls?" asked Lila.

"First, I practiced pouring melted wax into doll face molds. I tried reshaping the faces once the molded wax hardened. Some of my creations were pretty bad." Far Nana chuckled, remembering.

Rose picked up the wax brick. "Can we make something?"

"Sure, but practice with this. It will be easier to shape." Far Nana handed Rose a glob of softer wax in a plastic bag.

Rose pulled the wax from its bag. She and Lila tried mushing the wax into different nose shapes.

While they practiced, Far Nana washed the doll's dress and underwear. After she hung them up to dry, she said, "That's enough for today."

"Why don't you finish cleaning the rest of no-nose with alcohol?" asked Lila.

"I'll finish up tomorrow when I'm fresh," said Far Nana.

"I can't wait to find out how no-nose's nose fell off," said Rose. "Will you ask her now?"

When they'd first come to live with Far Nana, Rose and Lila had learned something amazing. Far Nana could talk to dolls. She could hear dolls and tell their stories. At first, Rose and Lila hadn't really believed it. But now they were pretty sure it was true. They hoped to learn how to do it someday, too.

Far Nana looked at her watch. "I think we have time for some of the story today." She got a flowered scarf from a drawer and draped it around the doll.

Lila curled up on the window seat. She held a hot-dog-shaped wax nose she had made against the tip of her own nose. "If no-nose tells us some lies, maybe she could grow a new, long Pinocchio nose."

Rose and Far Nana laughed. Far Nana set the doll on a pillow by the window and gazed into its blue-violet eyes. Pale rays of winter sunlight lit up its face. The light shone through the outer part of the wax, so the doll almost seemed to glow.

After a few seconds, Far Nana began to speak. And the doll's story began.

CHAPTER 5
❧ My Beginning ❧
Glory's Story

*M*y very first memory was a day in 1859 when the toy maker placed me in the window at the front of his London toy shop.

He rubbed his hands together in glee. "Right! When customers see you, they won't be able to resist coming inside my shop."

I stared at my reflection in the toy shop's glass window. I had blue-violet glass eyes. My cheeks and lips were painted pink. I wore a white ball gown covered with small purple and pink flowers. Embroidered ruffles along the bottom of my skirt were edged with purple velvet ribbon that matched my shoes.

The window was full of other dolls, toys, and a paper doll theater. Once the toy maker walked away, a bisque doll in a golden dress and a shiny crown spoke to me.

So you're finally finished, she said in a sharp voice. *It took a long time and a lot of skill to make you. What's your name, girl?*

I don't know, I said. *What's yours?*

The painted fortune-teller puppet hanging above me in the window chuckled. His wooden legs clacked together softly. *That's Queen Victoria, dearie. Who else would wear a crown all the time?*

Silence, you horrid puppet! demanded the queen. *You're a fine one to offer advice on fashion. Just look at you, wearing a turban and pointed elf shoes. And that ridiculous so-called crystal ball you carry. Really!*

I interrupted their squabbling to ask. *Where am I?*

You're in a toy shop, said the puppet.

The finest toy shop in all of London, added the queen.

And you are the finest doll the toy maker has ever made. He said so himself, chirped a tiny, excited voice. It was the Cinderella paper doll from the fairy tale theater.

Queen Victoria frowned.

The genie doll next to the puppet laughed. *I say! You're looking a bit green around the edges, Queen. Jealous of the new doll, perhaps?*

'Tis quite obvious you're a genie, not a genius, huffed the queen. *I am far more beautiful. The new doll is simply unusual.*

Why am I unusual? I asked.

You are the only wax doll in the shop. And you look almost real, Cinderella explained. *Even though the toy workshop is behind us, we can see inside it in the reflection in the window glass. So we watched you being made.*

Let me tell her! I could see best, said one of Cinderella's stepsister paper dolls. *The toy maker poured melted wax into plaster molds to make your head, arms, and legs.*

Cinderella's other stepsister butted in. *Your hair was the best part. Every single hair on your head was poked in —*

Please! said Queen Victoria. *Maybe she doesn't want to hear the gory details.*

No! Tell me, I said.

The stepsister continued. *Each hair was poked into your head one by one with a hot needle. Each of your eyelashes was added in the same way.*

They look very real, said the genie.

But did it hurt? worried Cinderella.

Not a bit, I said. *I don't remember any of it.*

Well, my favorite part was your beautiful clothes, said Cinderella. *First, came your linen and lace slip, then a corset, and —*

For shame! cried the queen. *Don't talk about underwear when there are gentlemen present.*

What gentlemen? asked Cinderella.

The puppet and the genie, to name two, hissed the queen.

Don't be so stuffy, Your Majesty, said the puppet. *Even gentlemen have heard of underwear, you know.*

Wear it myself, added the genie.

Don't forget to tell her how the toy maker bent thin strips of wood to form the round hoops of her hoopskirt, said one of the stepsisters.

And then he spent days making your gown and bonnet, said the other stepsister.

And here you are, said Cinderella. *Welcome to the toy shop.*

Thank you, I replied.

CHAPTER 6
❧ Customers ❧
Glory's Story

Just then, two ladies in fine gowns passed by outside on the street. They stared at us in our window and then came inside the shop.

"How much for the stunning doll in your window?" one of the ladies asked the toy maker.

The queen looked pleased, thinking the lady was describing her. But then the lady pointed at me!

The toy maker smiled but shook his head. "I am terribly sorry, madam. The wax doll is not for sale. It is only for display."

"How disappointing," said the lady. "She's quite unusual."

"Perhaps another doll?" suggested the toy maker. He showed her the other dolls and toys that filled the shop. There were dolls made of china, bisque, and papier-mâché. There were dollhouses, games, toy trains, rocking horses, marbles, and puzzles.

After shopping awhile, the lady's friend said, "Hurry, dear, we'll be late for tea."

The lady nodded and pointed to a china doll in our window. "I've made a choice. I will purchase this doll. It will look delightful in my sunroom."

Farewell! The paper dolls told the china doll when the toy maker took her away.

Cheerio! the genie added.

The puppet looked into his crystal ball. *Your future looks bright*, he called after the doll.

That was the last we saw of her. This is how I learned that the dolls in the shop were there to be sold. All except for me, that is. I realized that no matter how many friends I made, they would all be sold away sooner or later.

Over the following days, customers often came in to the shop, hoping to buy me. But the toy maker always said no. He showed them another toy or doll, and they usually found something else they liked.

The other dolls and I passed the time playing games. The paper dolls sometimes entertained us with songs. Though the queen complained that their notes were flat, I think she secretly enjoyed their music.

We took turns having the fortune-teller puppet look into his crystal ball and tell our futures.

One night, he told mine. He said: *I see two long jour-*

neys in your future, one by sea and one by land. You will have adventures. Then you will sleep for more than one hundred years, while holding the key to a dear friend's secret.

The paper dolls giggled.

Queen Victoria shuddered. *Dolls and adventure don't mix.*

Sometimes I wish something exciting would happen to me, I told the queen. *You and the others will be sold and go to new homes someday. But I will be here always.*

Don't be ungrateful, girl, said the queen. *The toy maker toiled for over a month creating you. The least you can do is bring customers into the shop. Just sit there and smile.*

I didn't mean to be ungrateful. I tried to follow the queen's advice. I sat and smiled day after day.

And I did help the toy maker bring in customers. Soon there were so many that he had to hire an assistant clerk for the shop.

I never got to know the new clerk. But I don't imagine he lasted long. On his first day, he made a mistake. A mistake so big that I'm sure the toy maker never forgave him.

CHAPTER 7
❧ The Mistake ❧
Glory's Story

*T*he new clerk's first day of work began like any other. I was chatting with the Cinderella paper doll.

Fine weather today, isn't it? I said.

Brrr! Maybe for a wax doll like you, said Cinderella. *But I'm freezing. My skin is paper thin!*

We giggled.

The fortune-teller puppet gazed into his crystal ball. *I see a tall, dark stranger coming,* he warned us.

We all see him, scoffed the queen. *He's right outside the window.*

I looked out. A gentleman wearing a long black coat and a tall black hat was coming toward the shop. Snowflakes swirled around him and dusted the cobblestone streets.

I say! What a handsome gentleman, said one of Cinderella's stepsisters.

I hope he comes inside. How do I look? asked the other stepsister.

Lovely as always. But do you think he'll notice me? asked the first stepsister.

Honestly! You paper dolls never stop chattering, said the queen.

The little bell on the door clink-clanked as the well-dressed gentleman came into our shop.

The new clerk rushed to greet him. He was alone in the shop. The toy maker had gotten a terrible toothache and had gone to a dentist.

"Welcome, sir! May I help you?"

"I wish to buy a gift for my niece," said the gentleman. "Something special — the most expensive doll you have."

The clerk's eyes sparkled. He hurried over to the window and lifted me from my spot. "This is the finest doll in the entire shop, it's poured wax —"

The gentleman waved his gloved hand to show he wasn't interested in hearing the details. "Yes, yes. I'm in a hurry. I'll take it."

I stared at the clerk in amazement.

Doesn't he know I'm not for sale? I wondered.

The toy maker left for the dentist's office in such a rush that he forgot to tell him, Cinderella said. She sounded upset.

The clerk turned me around and around. He even

30

looked inside my hat. "She doesn't seem to have a price tag," he told the gentleman. "Perhaps we should wait until the toy maker returns."

"I haven't time for that." The gentleman put a stack of money on the counter.

The clerk smiled greedily when he saw it. "I'm sure that will be more than enough, sir."

And just like that, I was sold!

"Pack the doll in a sturdy wooden crate. I plan to ship it to my niece in America," said the gentleman.

Where is America? I asked the other dolls.

It's a land far across the ocean, the genie said.

If only the toy maker would come back, said Cinderella. *He would stop the clerk from selling you.*

But this was my chance to escape. Oh, hurry, gentleman, I thought. Take me away before the toy maker returns.

The clerk placed me in a wooden crate full of straw.

Bon voyage! said the queen. She sounded glad I was leaving.

Cheerio! Good-bye! called the other dolls.

Be careful, Cinderella warned me. *There's danger out there.*

Farewell, I called back. *Don't worry about me.*

The reflection of the puppet's face in the shop window was the last thing I saw. He winked as he whispered, *And so begins your first journey.*

Bam! Bam! Bam! The crate was nailed shut with me inside.

There were long cracks between the wooden boards of my crate that allowed me to see out. The gentleman carried me from the shop to the end of the street. There, we got in a carriage and traveled to the boat docks beside the Thames River.

The gentleman took me inside a station. "I have a package bound for America," he told someone. "Address it to my niece, Miss Arabella Cornelius, at the Cornelius Plantation in Alabama."

I was tossed into a room where I waited among other boxes for a while. Soon I was loaded onto a boat, which sailed that very afternoon. The next day I was moved onto a larger ship full of cargo, which set sail across the Atlantic Ocean.

Weeks passed. I lay in the dark silence of the cargo ship and listened to it creak and moan as the ocean rocked it. My corset was tight, and the straw itched my nose.

Sometimes fierce winter storms raged outside, and I was a little scared. Salt water seeped into the cargo area and sloshed around the boxes below me.

On calmer days, I felt lonely. I wondered what Cinderella and the others were doing back in the toy shop.

Hello! I called out one day, wondering if another doll

might be traveling in one of the other boxes. But there was no answer.

After a long voyage, the ship reached America and I was unloaded. I journeyed by train, then stagecoach, and then I was placed on a wagon.

I began to wonder if I would ever get to where I was going.

One morning, the wagon turned up a long driveway. I peeked between the cracks in my crate. Tangled gray moss hung from tall oak trees that lined the path.

At the end of the driveway, the wagon lurched to a stop. Had my trip ended at last?

CHAPTER 8
◆ Invitation ◆

Riiing! Far Nana stopped mid-story.

Lila popped out of her chair. "The phone! I'll get it!" She ran out the door of the witch's hat, leaving Far Nana and Rose behind.

When Lila didn't come back right away, Far Nana called down the hall. "Who is it?"

"Next-door Nadia," Lila yelled back. Nadia was a girl who lived in the house next to Far Nana's. She was in Rose's fourth-grade class.

"Okay," said Far Nana. She sat back down.

"I wonder what Nadia wants?" said Rose.

Just then, Lila ran back to the witch's hat, looking excited. "Can Nadia sleep over tomorrow night?"

"On a school night?" Far Nana asked doubtfully. "Tomorrow is Sunday."

"Yeah, I know," said Lila. "But Nadia's mother has to go out of town for her job. Her mom tried to get a baby-sitter, but she couldn't find one. And Nadia can't stay home all alone. So can she sleep over here? Please, please, please?"

Far Nana thought for a minute. Then she said, "Tell Nadia to tell her mother that we'll be glad to help out. Nadia is welcome to spend the night."

"Yay!" Lila dashed back down the hall. Rose and Far Nana heard her yell into the phone, "Far Nana said yes!"

Rose thought Lila would come back, but she just kept on laughing and talking to Nadia. What was so funny? Rose felt left out.

Far Nana got a book from a shelf and showed it to Rose. It had pictures of dolls inside. "Maybe you can help me choose a new nose for Ms. Tate's doll, since Lila's busy."

While Far Nana flipped pages, Rose tried to over-hear Lila. She wanted to help choose the doll's new nose, but she also wanted to know what Lila and Nadia were saying.

Far Nana showed Rose pictures of several old wax dolls in the book. "I could make a new nose for the doll like any of these. Which one do you think would look best on her?"

Rose studied the noses one by one, trying to imagine each nose on the doll's face. Finally, she pointed at a small, cute nose. "This one?"

Far Nana looked at the doll nose Rose had chosen.

"I like it, too. So that's the nose I'll make, then." She saved the page with a bookmark.

"Better not tell Lila we've been picking noses," Rose warned. "She'll start making jokes about doll boogers."

Far Nana laughed. "It'll be our secret."

When Lila came back again, they all went downstairs for supper. On the way, Rose asked, "What were you and Nadia talking about?"

Lila shrugged. "I don't know. Stuff. I can't wait 'til she sleeps over tomorrow night, can you?"

"No, I guess not," said Rose.

"What's wrong?" asked Lila. "Don't you like Nadia?"

"I like her," said Rose. The real question, Rose thought, was: Did Nadia like her — or just Lila?

After supper, they all went back to the witch's hat, where the doll's story continued.

CHAPTER 9
❖ My New Home ❖
Glory's Story

Through a hole in my crate, I could see we had stopped alongside a magnificent two-story white mansion. Pink and purple flowers wound up six tall columns across the front of the house.

A young girl with blond ringlet curls ran out of the house toward me. "What's in the box? Is it for me?" she shouted at the wagon driver.

A dark-skinned woman ran out of the house after her. "Stay out of the sun, Miz Arabella. Your mama won't like it if you get freckles."

"Oh, Millie. You always worry," said the girl. "The sun's not hot enough to give me freckles. It's the middle of winter."

Their soft voices sounded different from the sharp London voices I was used to hearing.

The wagon driver lifted my crate from the wagon. "Package for Miss Arabella Cornelius," he said.

"That's me!" Arabella jumped up and down, clapping her hands with excitement.

Arabella was the gentleman's niece! I had arrived in Alabama at the Cornelius Plantation at last. The driver unloaded my crate and carried me to the porch steps.

"You stay on this porch out of the sun now, Miz Arabella," said Millie. "I can't watch you every minute and I got work to do." She headed back inside the house.

Snap! Snap! Snap! The driver opened my crate. Then I heard his footsteps and the creak of wagon wheels as he continued on his journey.

Arabella's small hands dug through the straw and lifted me into the sunlight.

"What ya got, Bella?" A girl about Arabella's age skipped across the porch toward us. Her skin was brown like Millie's, and she wore a simple cotton dress.

"Come look, May," called Arabella. "It's a present from my uncle Winston — all the way from England!"

May sat beside Arabella on the steps. She smiled when she saw me. "A doll!"

Arabella frowned.

"Is it Queen Victoria? The doll you wanted?" asked May.

"Don't you know anything?" said Arabella. "Queens wear crowns. My uncle sent me the wrong doll."

"But this doll is pretty anyway," said May. "Don't you like her?"

"I wanted a Queen Victoria doll. Phooey," Arabella pushed me off her lap onto the step.

May picked me up and touched my black curls with wonder. "You could just call her Victoria and pretend she's a queen."

"No!" said Arabella. "Someday my uncle will send me the right doll. I can't have two Victorias."

"What's her name, then?" asked May.

"I don't know." Arabella sounded bored.

A cool breeze blew one of the pink flowers winding up the porch columns onto my skirt.

May picked it up with one hand. She brushed it back and forth below her nose as she gazed at me. "You could name her Glory, after these mornin' glory flowers your mama planted."

Arabella sighed. "Glory's good enough, I suppose."

"I spy somethin' blue," said May.

"What?" said Arabella. "Oh, we're playing I Spy?" She looked around for something blue.

"The ribbons on my dress?" Arabella guessed.

May grinned, but shook her head no.

"My eyes?" Arabella guessed.

"No," said May. "You're gettin' warmer though."

"I give up," said Arabella.

"It's you! You're feelin' blue because you didn't get

40

the doll you wanted. Only now you're not so blue because I 'I Spyed' you out of it," said May.

Arabella giggled.

"Arabella, honey. Get out of the sun. You're going to freckle," called a pale, blond woman from the doorway behind us. "Where's Millie? She should be watching over you better than this."

Arabella snatched me away from May and hurried to show me to the woman. "Mama," she complained. "Uncle Winston sent me the wrong doll from England. Will you write him a letter and ask him to send Queen Victoria instead?"

Her mother patted Arabella's blond curls. "Of course, darlin'. I'm sure he simply didn't know. But this doll is pretty, too." Then she took a closer look at me. "Oh, my. What was your uncle thinking? She's made of wax!"

Arabella frowned at me. "What's wrong with wax?"

Good question, I thought. What *was* wrong with being made of wax?

"We'll discuss it later, darlin'," said her mother. "I'll ask your uncle to send you the doll you want." She looked at me again. "Before summer comes."

CHAPTER 10
❧ May's Idea ❧
Glory's Story

*H*urry along now. We've got to practice your piano and then your reading," Arabella's mother told her.

"How come? Practice time isn't until afternoon," said Arabella.

"Our neighbors are coming to visit from the Plum Plantation tomorrow, and I want to show them what a little lady you are."

"Oh, no! Not that dumb Prudence Plum," said Arabella.

"She's a perfectly nice girl. Now that you're growing up, you need to make more friends of your own kind," her mother said. She glanced at May with dislike. "You won't learn good manners from slaves."

Arabella's mother handed me to May. "Take this doll to Arabella's room, child. And don't dawdle."

"Yes, missus," said May. We followed Arabella and her mother through the tall, double front doors.

Inside the house, maids were polishing the oak floors. A footman on a ladder was shining a chandelier with candles that hung from the high ceiling.

"Come on, Arabella. Into the parlor," said Arabella's mother. They disappeared into a room on the first floor.

May carried me up a wide staircase and down a long hall on the second floor of the house.

She turned me this way and that to look at the paintings hanging on the hall walls. "All these folks are Bella's family, Glory. All dead now, though."

Halfway down the hall, she stopped in front of a painting of a man with a patch over one eye. "Except this one. This is the Master, Bella's daddy." She shivered.

May continued down the hall and went into a bedroom. She set me on a bed with a blue ruffled canopy and stood back to smile at me. "This is Arabella's bedroom. It's your room now, too, I reckon."

She got two dolls from a doll buggy near the window and brought them to the bed. "Just so you won't be lonely, here are some friends for you. This corn husk doll is Netty. I made her for Arabella after the last corn harvest. And this china doll is Lou Ann."

"This here is Glory," she told the other two dolls. "She's new. She came in a box from a far away place called England."

She arranged the dolls on either side of me.

Then May leaned close to me and whispered. "Someday, I'm gonna do some travelin' just like you. I've got a plan. And you gave me the idea this very day. But we can't tell. Not even Bella."

And then May was gone.

CHAPTER 11
❧ Doll Talk ❧
Glory's Story

I could see myself in the silver-framed wall mirror across from the bed. The other two dolls' reflections stared at me in the mirror.

What was May whispering to you? asked Netty.

You shouldn't eavesdrop, Netty, scolded Lou Ann.

What do you expect? asked Netty. *I'm made out of corn. So naturally I'm all ears.*

Lou Ann and Netty giggled like old friends.

Don't mind Netty, Lou Ann told me. *Welcome to the big house.*

Where's the big house? I asked.

You're in it. We live in the big house, said Lou Ann. *So do Arabella and her mama. And the Master, Arabella's daddy.*

Does May live here, too? I asked.

Netty giggled. *No, silly. May is a slave. She lives in a cabin near the kitchen with the other house slaves. The Mas-*

ter keeps them close by, so they can be called to the big house to do cleaning, washing, mending, and such.

Arabella doesn't have any brothers or sisters. That's why Arabella's mama lets her play with May, Lou Ann explained. *May does a lot of work, but her main job is to be Arabella's friend.*

Like us, I said.

Right, said Netty.

Where are May's mother and father? I asked.

I don't know. They got sold away before I came, said Lou Ann.

I knew dolls were sold. But I didn't know people were, I said in surprise.

Not all people. Only slaves, said Netty.

How many slaves live here? I asked.

The Master owns about twelve house slaves. And lots more field slaves live in cabins farther away from the big house, said Lou Ann. *They pick the cotton when it's ready every November. Plowing and planting will start in a month or so. Spring's coming. Soon it will be warmer.*

Warmer than this? I thought. I already felt droopy. It had been snowing when I left London. It wasn't nearly as cold here in Alabama, even though it was still winter.

CHAPTER 12
❖ Visitors ❖
Glory's Story

*T*he next morning, May woke Arabella and me up bright and early. "Mornin', Bella. Mornin', Glory."

"Morning," mumbled Arabella.

Good morning, I answered.

May poured water into a blue-and-white china bowl on top of the dresser. Arabella washed her face and hands in the bowl. Then she brushed her teeth.

May rushed around, helping Arabella get dressed. First, she helped her put on lacey pantalettes, then petticoats, and then her dress and shoes.

Arabella just stood there, yawning, while May did all the work.

"Hurry now, Bella. Company will be here soon," said May.

"Phooey! Who cares about that dumb Pru Plum from the Plum Plantation. Let's play marbles until she gets here," said Arabella. "I'll meet you after breakfast."

"Okay. Bring Glory, too," said May.

"Who's Glory?" asked Arabella.

May looked surprised. "Your new doll."

Arabella giggled. "Oh, I forgot."

Arabella took me downstairs to breakfast. She set me on an empty chair next to her at a long, polished wooden table.

Her father stared at me with his one good eye — the one without the patch. "What in tarnation is that doll doing at the table?"

"Uncle Winston sent her," said Arabella.

Her father grumbled a little and went on eating. Brown-skinned slaves rushed to and fro, serving breakfast. They brought eggs, sausages, potatoes, cheese, bread and butter, buckwheat pancakes with syrup, and tea. All that, for just Arabella and her parents.

After breakfast, we left the house and went past several wagons near the horse stables. Slaves were packing shipping crates with items made on the plantation and loading them onto a wagon for sale in town.

We passed a dairy, a weaving room, and a gardener's hut. There were slaves working in each building. Arabella looked for May everywhere.

We headed inside a workroom full of wax for making candles and soap. For a moment, I felt right at home. But May wasn't there, so we continued on.

Arabella ducked into a brick building with smoke coming from its chimney. Millie was inside, stirring one of several pots cooking in the big fireplace. The room was full of trays, serving bowls, and all kinds of food. It smelled spicy.

Millie waved her arms at us. "Shoo! Out of the kitchen. I got lots of cookin' to do before the company comes today."

"Where's May?" asked Arabella.

"Out back, gettin' water," said Millie.

We went around to the yard behind the kitchen. May was lifting a heavy bucket full of water.

"Be right back," she told us.

When May returned, she pulled some small, hard clay balls from her pocket. "Made some new marbles last night."

"Let's play Ringer," said Arabella, grabbing the marbles. She tossed me near a tree, where I lay forgotten in the bright sunshine.

May nodded. "Draw the circle right quick, will you?"

Arabella found a stick and began drawing a big circle with an X in the middle in the dirt. She placed marbles along the X. While she was busy, May walked over to me. She set me up straight in the shade of the tree and fluffed my skirts so they formed a neat circle around me.

"There. That's better," she said. "Now you can watch our game."

She went back to Arabella and their game began. They took turns shooting marbles into the ring, trying

to knock the marbles on the X outside of the ring. I wasn't sure, but I thought May let Arabella win. Just to keep her happy.

Sometime later, I heard a carriage pull up in the driveway. A footman helped a lady, a gentleman, and a girl about Arabella's age get out of the carriage.

Arabella and May peeked at them from behind my tree.

"Oh! Pru looks prettier than I remember," said Arabella.

"Company's here, Miz Arabella," Millie called. "Get on up to the big house."

Arabella grabbed May's hand. "Let's go."

May pulled away. "Not me. Your mama wouldn't like it. I'll take Glory upstairs. Then I have to help Millie serve the company."

CHAPTER 13
❖ Getting Warmer ❖
Glory's Story

*M*ay took me to Arabella's room and left in a hurry. A few hours later, Arabella came upstairs with Pru. May wasn't with them.

Pru walked around Arabella's bedroom picking things up without asking, then setting them down like they weren't interesting. Arabella was right. Pru was pretty. She had red curls and she was wearing a frilly pink dress. But she didn't act pretty.

She finally picked me up. "Who's this?"

"My new doll. It's from London," Arabella said. "I don't like it. May does, though."

"Your slave girl? Who cares what she thinks?" said Pru.

"Not me," said Arabella.

Just then, May stepped inside the door. She was carrying a tray of lemonade and snacks. I hoped she hadn't heard Arabella and Pru.

Bang! May set the tray on a small table. She *had* heard!

"So you like Arabella's new doll?" Pru asked May.

May looked mad, but she nodded stiffly. "Yes, Miz Pru. I like Miz Arabella's new doll."

"You haven't seen my Queen Victoria doll," said Pru. "Now *it's* pretty. Got it for my ninth birthday. At my party, I wore a queen dress and a golden crown. I had a cake as big as a carriage wheel with nine candles and pink frosting."

"Lucky you. I wanted a Queen Victoria. But my uncle sent me this doll by mistake," said Arabella.

Pru poked me with a long, hard, pointy finger. She left a tiny fingernail dent in my nose. "This doll sure is funny-looking."

"It's made of wax," said Arabella.

Pru's eyes got big as she stared at me. She smiled a sneaky grin as she set me back on the bed. "I have an idea. Let's play I Spy. You can play, too, May."

"No, thank you," said May.

"You're a slave, so you have to do what we say. Tell her, Arabella," said Pru.

"Come on, May," said Arabella. "Let's all play together. It'll be fun."

May didn't really have a choice. She *did* have to do what the other girls said. "Yes, Miz Arabella," she said.

"I spy something that melts," Pru announced.

"That's easy," said Arabella. "The candle."

Pru shook her head. "No."

"Oh! I know," said Arabella. "The taffy. Or the fudge." She pointed at the food tray on the table near me.

"Wrong again," said Pru. "But you're getting warmer. What do you guess, May?"

May shrugged and looked at what else was on the tray. "The honey popcorn balls?"

"You're getting hot," said Pru. "I'll give you another hint. It has a tiny hat and a flowered dress."

All three girls looked at me.

I heard Netty and Lou Ann gasp from their doll buggy by the window.

"My new doll?" asked Arabella.

"That's it!" said Pru.

"Dolls don't melt," said Arabella.

"I stayed in London all last summer. A London summer isn't hot enough to melt a wax doll. But a plantation summer is," insisted Pru.

So that's why Arabella's mother had acted like there was something wrong with wax, I realized in horror.

May hurried over to hug me. "She's right, Glory! Oh, no —"

Pru leaned over us. "Oh, yessss!" she hissed. "*Drip, drip! Ssss!* This doll is going to melt right into a puddle."

May jumped up and stared hard at Pru. Before she could stop herself, she said, "I spy somethin' mean."

Pru's jaw dropped. "Are you calling *me* mean?"

May stepped back, looking scared. "No, Miz Pru. I wasn't —"

"I'm telling. You'll be sorry for talking to me like that. Just you wait." Pru stomped out the door.

"Now look what you've done!" Arabella shouted at May. "She's mad and she'll tell my daddy on you. He'll make you work out in the fields!"

May looked worried. "She *is* mean, though."

"But you can't tell her that. You're only a slave," said Arabella.

"Why are you takin' her side? You like her better than me?" asked May.

"Well, I — Mama told me to be nice to her, that's all." Arabella ran after Pru.

After she left, May gave me another quick hug. "Poor Glory. You need to run away from here even more than I do. Before you melt."

I couldn't believe it. Instead of worrying about getting in trouble with Arabella's daddy, May was worried about me!

I was worried about me, too.

That night as Arabella slept, I sat on the end of her bed. I was afraid to sleep. I might melt into a puddle and never wake up again.

I remembered what Lou Ann had said: *Spring's coming. Soon it will be warmer.*

CHAPTER 14
❖ Melting ❖
Glory's Story

"B̶et you can't guess where we're going," Arabella whispered to me later that night. She wrapped herself in a warm cloak. "Daddy says May has to be a field slave from now on. Just because she back-talked Pru. May's mad about that, but maybe she'll feel better if I bring you along to see her."

Arabella lit a candle to light our way. We tiptoed down the stairs and sneaked out of the house. Beyond some shadowed azalea bushes, we came to a group of small log cabins that all looked alike.

Arabella opened the door to one of the cabins without knocking. There was no one inside.

We heard voices coming closer. Arabella blew out the candle, went into the cabin, and hid behind on old wood table.

Millie, May, and an old man walked in. Millie began gathering some things together. May pulled something small and square from under a sleeping pallet on the floor. Was it a book?

"Field work is no life for a smart girl like May," said Millie. "I don't want her to work in the cotton fields from sunup to sundown 'til the day she dies."

"I was goin' to escape on the Underground Railroad tonight, but May can take my place," said an old man.

"No, Uncle Louis," said May.

The old man patted her hand. "Child, the escape plan was your idea anyway. It's fair that you should get to go."

May seemed sad and happy at the same time as she hugged her uncle. "All right. Thank you."

Arabella gasped. Everyone turned to look at us.

"Shush! There's Miz Arabella!" Millie warned.

"What are you doing here?" May asked us. Millie and the old man slipped outside, leaving the cabin door slightly open.

Arabella stood slowly. "What were they talking about, May? What's the Underground Railroad?"

May looked scared.

"It's a runaway railroad for slaves, isn't it?" demanded Arabella.

"Y-yes," said May.

"Where did you get money to buy a ticket?" asked Arabella.

"It's not a real railroad with real trains. It's a long

trail that goes north—to freedom. Millie says there are hiding places and people along the way to help," said May.

"Don't go. Who will I play with?" whined Arabella.

"We're friends now, Bella. But someday you're gonna grow up. Then what happens?" said May.

"We'll still be friends."

"The way Millie is friends with your mama? Your mama is the boss, and Millie has to do what she says. Someday you'll be a missus with a husband and house to take care of. And I'll still be your slave to boss around," said May.

"It won't be like that," promised Arabella.

May stared at her. "Will to. You're already changin'. Now you're not nice to me when your other friends come around."

Arabella's fingers squeezed my arm. She was getting mad. "If you try to leave, I'll tell Daddy. He pays money for slaves like you. So if you run away, that's like stealing from my family."

"You do that, and your daddy will hurt me for tryin' to go to freedom," said May. "Please don't tell."

Suddenly, the cabin door banged all the way open.

"What in thunder are you doing out here in the middle of the night?" barked a man's deep voice.

Arabella and May jumped. As Arabella whirled toward the door, I flew from her hand. I skidded across

the cabin's hard dirt floor and landed at the edge of the fireplace.

Something tickled my nose. It began to sting. And burn. I had fallen on a hot coal. My nose was melting!

"Daddy?" Arabella said to the one-eyed man towering in the doorway.

"You scared your mama half to death when she couldn't find you in bed. Get into the house!" he roared at Arabella. "I'll deal with you later."

Without another word, Arabella disappeared into the darkness outside. She was going back to the big house — without me!

Arabella's father pointed a long finger at May. "And as for you. You're the one who back-talked Prudence Plum. And now you got my Arabella sneaking around at night. I don't need troublemakers on my plantation. You're headed for the auction block come tomorrow."

CHAPTER 15
❦ Wondering ❦

Far Nana yawned and stretched. "That's all for to-night."

"You can't stop now!" said Rose.

"You always stop at the most exciting parts," complained Lila.

"There's never a good stopping place," said Far Nana. She shooed them off to their room.

After they got in bed, Rose and Lila each opened the lockets they wore. They kissed the pictures of their parents inside like they did every night.

"Do you think May will get sold at an auction like those dolls this morning?" Lila asked from the top bunk.

"I hope not," Rose said. "But maybe. I learned at school that they used to sell slaves like that."

They both fell asleep, wondering.

CHAPTER 16
❖ Snow Day ❖

Up and at 'em," Far Nana called early the next morning. Then she went down the hall, whistling cheerfully.

Rose groaned and pulled the bedcovers over her head. "Why does she say 'Up and Adam' every morning to wake us up?"

"Yeah. Who's Adam anyway?" grumbled Lila from the bunk above Rose.

Their grandmother came back and stood in their bedroom doorway. "Come on, girls. Up and at 'em."

Rose opened one eye. Her grandmother was wearing a bright orange dress with flowers on it, and lots of beaded necklaces. Rose closed her eye. Bright orange was too hard to look at at seven in the morning.

"It's Sunday," said Rose. "No school. So tell Adam we don't have to get up early."

"Who's Adam?" Far Nana asked.

"Good question," said Lila.

"I thought you girls would be excited about getting up on a snow day," said Far Nana.

"Snow day?" Rose hurried out of bed and over to look out the window.

Lila slid down the bunk bed ladder. "Brrr! The floor is freezing cold!" She hopped across the floor to stand beside Rose.

Outside, the falling snow was so thick they couldn't even see the sidewalk below. Their breath made two fog circles on the inside of the window glass.

"Sunday can't be a snow day," Rose told Far Nana. "Snow days are when you stay home from school because of snow."

"Well, it's a day. And it's snowing," said Far Nana. "I call that a snow day. Let's celebrate with some snowman pancakes."

Down in the kitchen, Far Nana poured three small circles of batter to make a snowman. She added raisins for the eyes, nose, and mouth. She made one for Rose and one for Lila.

After breakfast, Lila peeked outside. "It's still snowing hard."

"When it stops, you can go out," said Far Nana. "For now, I'm making hot chocolate with cinnamon. Then I'm going up to the witch's hat to work on Glory. Any takers?"

"Me!" said Rose.

"Me!" said Lila.

Meow! said Far Nana's four cats, Ringo, John, George, and Paul. They wound around Far Nana's, Rose's, and Lila's legs as the three of them went upstairs.

Inside the witch's hat, Rose and Lila snuggled under knitted blankets, licked their cinnamon sticks, and sipped hot cocoa. They watched Far Nana work.

Far Nana lay Glory on the table and got the scissors. "I don't want to get wax on Glory's body, since it's made of cloth. So before I clean the wax head, arms, and legs, I'm going to snip the threads holding them onto the body."

Rose set down her hot chocolate. "Can I do it?"

"Sure. There are two threads on each arm, two on each leg, two on the front of the shoulders, and two on the back." Far Nana handed her the scissors.

Rose snipped carefully.

"Let me do some," said Lila.

Rose let Lila snip the leg threads. After they finished, Far Nana set the doll's cloth body aside.

Outside the witch's hat, the snowstorm blew harder than ever. Wind rattled the windows. Every now and then tiny balls of hail tapped on the glass.

Rose and Lila sat back and sipped their cocoa while Far Nana cleaned the doll's wax face, arms, and legs with alcohol.

Then she began making a new nose for Glory. She

put a small piece of yellowish wax into a metal bowl and added colored wax crayon shavings. Next, she heated the bowl over a little flame until all the wax melted.

Once the wax had cooled, she got to work shaping it into a nose. She used sharp, wooden-handled tools with curved or pointed metal ends.

A while later, Far Nana got out a blow dryer. She pointed it toward Glory's partly made nose.

"Are you going to blow her nose?" Rose joked.

Far Nana laughed. "The blow dryer's heat will keep the wax soft as I work it."

It took a long time to shape Glory's nose exactly right. Finally, Far Nana set the new nose on Glory's face. She warmed the wax with the blow dryer again. Then she smoothed it with her fingers until the nose was attached.

"What do you think?" Far Nana asked when she was done.

"It looks like she was made that way to begin with," said Lila.

"It looks good," said Rose.

"That's what I was hoping you'd say." Far Nana turned on the blow dryer once more. This time, she aimed it at one of Glory's arms. She rubbed the back of the round part of a metal spoon in circles on Glory's arm.

When she was done, Rose looked closely at the arm. "The tiny cracks are gone!"

"Warm air from the blow dryer softens the wax enough to smooth away small cracks. While I fix the rest of Glory's cracks, will you girls work on shoveling the front stairs?" asked Far Nana. "The snow has stopped."

CHAPTER 17
❖ This Means War ❖

Rose and Lila looked out the window. Outside, snow covered the rooftops and street. Icicles dripped from the trees. Only a few lonely snowflakes still floated through the air like tiny feathers.

"It's beautiful," said Rose.

"Yay!" said Lila. "Let's go."

They ran downstairs and put on their jackets, scarves, and hats as fast as they could. Then they dashed out the door.

Splat! Splat! Two snowballs barely missed Rose and Lila as they stepped off the porch into the front yard.

"It's Nadia!" said Lila. "She's bombing us from next door!"

Lila dove behind a row of snow-covered bushes. Nadia was making more snowballs in her yard.

"This means war!" called Lila. She started making her own snowballs.

Splat! Splat!

"C'mon, Rose! Help!" Lila yelled.

"No fair. Two against one!" Nadia shouted.

Did that mean Nadia didn't want her to play? Rose wondered. Probably not. She and Nadia got along okay at school. But just in case, she didn't join the game. Instead, she got a shovel and began shoveling the porch steps. Maybe Lila or Nadia would ask her to play again.

Splat! Splat! Lila and Nadia kept tossing snowballs. They forgot all about Rose.

"Give up?" Lila yelled.

"No way," said Nadia.

Their snowball fight lasted until Nadia's mother called Nadia in to get her sleepover stuff. When Nadia ran inside her house, Lila went with her.

What am I — invisible or something? Rose wondered. She kept shoveling the stairs. Alone.

And nobody cared.

CHAPTER 18
❖ Moods ❖

A few minutes later, Nadia came back out with her overnight bag. Lila was carrying her sleeping bag. "C'mon, Rose," called Lila.

Rose put the shovel away and tagged along behind the other two girls into Far Nana's.

After they took off their wet jackets, sweaters, and hats, Far Nana put their sweaters into the dryer.

Then all three girls went up to the second floor.

"Cool room!" said Nadia when she saw their bedroom.

"It used to be our mom's," said Rose.

"Far Nana is our mom's mother, so our mom lived here when she was a kid, too," said Lila.

Nadia jumped up. "I've never been inside such a cool house. Can we go look around?"

Lila jumped up, too. "Yeah. Come on. The living room is extra cool."

Nadia hurried out of their bedroom and downstairs

after Lila. Rose followed behind them, wishing she had gotten to show Nadia around first.

Rose pushed through the long strings of beads hanging in the living room doorway. Lila was already opening a trunk Far Nana used as a table for plants. She was showing Nadia some of their grandmother's best stuff.

"This is where Far Nana keeps a lot of her junk from the olden days." Lila pointed at different stacks. "Games and books. Letters. Love beads. Her peace sign hat."

Nadia pulled out some glittery purple bellbottom pants and a purple tie-dyed T-shirt. Then she found an old green phone with a big round-holed dialer. "Your grandmother has way cooler old stuff than my mom does."

Lila nodded. "Far Nana used to be a hippie."

Nadia picked up a box from the bottom of the trunk. "What's this?"

"This old ring is sooo weird. Try it." Lila opened the box and pulled out a ring with a clear-colored jewel. She handed the ring to Nadia.

Nadia slipped it on. "Hey! It's turning blue-green."

"It's just a trick ring," said Rose. "Body heat makes it change colors."

"The different colors show how you're feeling," said Lila. She read the chart on the ring's box. "Blue-green means you're calm."

Nadia handed the ring back to Lila. "You do it."

Lila slipped it on and watched along with Nadia and Rose as the stone change to dark blue-purple.

Nadia read the ring box's chart. "Blue-purple means you're happy."

Lila smiled a big smile showing lots of teeth. "Yep. I lo-o-ove sleepovers." She took off the ring and gave it to Rose. "Your turn."

Rose put the ring on. It turned golden.

Lila read the box. "Golden means you're worried."

Rose snatched the ring off. "Worried? Me? I'm not worried."

But she was. She was worried that Nadia was starting to like Lila more than her. Nadia should be *her* friend. After all, they were in the same class.

Lila always made friends easier than Rose. It wasn't fair.

CHAPTER 19
❖ Friends ❖

The next morning, Far Nana woke them all up for school. "Up and at 'em."

"Who's Adam?" Nadia mumbled from her sleeping bag.

Lila yawned. "That's Far Nana talk for 'get up'."

"I'm going to work in the witch's hat now," Far Nana told them. "Breakfast is in the kitchen. Help yourself." She disappeared down the hall.

The three girls got dressed and went down to breakfast.

Nadia shivered. "Where's my sweater?"

"I think it's still in the dryer with ours," said Rose. "I'll get it."

Rose met Lila and Nadia in the kitchen a minute later. "Our things were still a little wet. So I left them in the dryer and turned it on again."

After breakfast, Rose pulled their clothes out of the dryer.

They slipped on their sweaters and jackets in a hurry. Then they headed off for school.

On the way, Lila saw some kids from her second-grade class. "Hey, Kelly! Ginger! Wait up!" she called. The two girls waved and slowed down. Lila ran ahead to walk with them. Rose and Nadia stayed behind and walked by themselves.

"Ms. Bean's starting our oral book reports today. What book are you doing yours on?" Nadia asked Rose.

"A mystery," said Rose. "But my report isn't until Wednesday."

"Lucky! Mine's today. I'm doing —" began Nadia.

"I'm doing *Super Classroom Knock-knock Jokes*," butted in a boy walking behind them. It was Bart. He was in Ms. Bean's class with them.

"Knock-knock," said Bart.

"Who's there?" asked Nadia.

"Banana," said Bart.

"Banana who?" asked Nadia.

"I already know this one," said Rose. "You're going to keep saying banana. Then you'll say 'orange' and Nadia will say 'orange who?' Then you'll say —"

"Orange you glad I didn't say banana?" said Bart.

Rose and Nadia groaned.

"I've heard that one a million times," said Rose.

"Me, too," said Nadia. "Don't you know any better ones?"

Bart told more knock-knock jokes all the way to school. When they got there, the three of them headed for class. A bunch of other kids were already inside their classroom, hanging up coats and backpacks.

Nadia took off her jacket and turned to hang it on a wall hook.

Bart started laughing and pointing.

What was so funny? Rose looked to see.

Oh, no! On the back of Nadia's sweater, hung a pair of big orange Far Nana underwear.

"I see London. I see France. I see Nadia's GIANT underpants," teased Bart.

"What?" asked Nadia.

The other kids gathered around to look.

"Static cling," said Rose, pointing like crazy. "There's underwear on your back. It must have gotten stuck there in the dryer."

Nadia turned red. She tried to snatch off the underwear. It kept trying to stick to her.

A girl named Kiko giggled. "Attack of Planet Underwear."

"Oh where, oh where is Nadia's underwear?" sang a boy named Michael.

Rose froze for a second. She felt sorry for Nadia. But if she tried to help, the other kids might make fun of her, too. Just sit down and stay out of it, she told herself. It's Nadia's problem.

But then she heard herself say: "It's for my book report."

The minute she said it, it felt right.

She rushed over to Nadia and grabbed the underwear. "Thanks. I was wondering where those were."

She pulled the underwear on over her pants. "I'm doing my report on the book about the principal who runs around in his underwear," she announced.

The other kids stared and giggled.

Bart leaned over to Michael and said loudly: "Knock-knock."

"Who's there?" asked Michael.

"Orange," said Bart.

"Orange who?" asked Michael.

Bart grinned. "Orange you glad you don't have *GIANT* orange underwear?"

Everyone laughed.

Their teacher, Ms. Bean, came in. She looked surprised to see Rose wearing the big underwear. "What's up?"

"They're for my book report," said Rose.

Ms. Bean smiled. "Very creative. But save them 'til it's report time."

Rose took the underwear off as fast as she could. She had been planning to do her report on a different book. But she had read the underwear book already. She would check it out of the library and reread some of it before Wednesday. Changing her report would be a snap.

Rose stuffed the underwear in her jacket pocket and then took her jacket off.

Bart began giggling again. Only this time, he was pointing at Rose!

Nadia ran over and peeled a static-cling gym sock off of Rose's sweater. It crackled and the threads stood up, reaching toward Rose.

"Static cling," Nadia said.

She showed the sock to Ms. Bean. "I'm doing my report on a book about sock-er."

Ms. Bean laughed. Nadia and Rose smiled at each other.

What a relief! thought Rose. She and Nadia *were* friends — the kind that stuck together.

CHAPTER 20
❖ Finishing Up ❖

When Rose and Lila got home from school that day, Far Nana called them upstairs. "Ms. Tate is coming over soon. Glory's all put back together. But I still have to finish untangling and curling her hair. And we've got to finish her story."

Rose and Lila dropped their backpacks, grabbed snacks, and dashed upstairs to sit on their favorite chairs in the witch's hat.

Far Nana took a deep breath. Then she began to comb Glory's hair with slow strokes. And Glory's story continued.

CHAPTER 21
❧ Danger ❧
Glory's Story

As I lay on the hot coals, I could almost hear Cinderella from the toy shop warning: *There's danger out there.*

She had been right.

Small brown hands lifted me gently from the fire. May! She cradled me close to her chest. "Oh, Glory. Your nose melted off!"

"Hurry up, May," warned Millie. "It's time to go."

"I'm runnin' away," May told me. "I can't leave you behind to melt this summer. So I guess you're runnin' away, too."

May followed Millie to a wagon with several big shipping crates in the back. Millie pulled the contents out of one crate. The old man from the cabin took the cargo she had removed in to the nearby woods and hid it there.

May got inside the empty wooden crate with me and lay down. "It's only right that you get to come along," she told me. "Because you gave me the idea for how to escape, remember? We're leavin' the same way you came. In a box."

Millie set a package of food and a jar of water beside May. She tearfully kissed her cheek. Then she covered us with straw and closed the crate's lid.

Bam! Bam! Bam! The old man hammered the crate shut.

"Have a safe journey," Millie whispered to us from outside the crate.

"Bye, Millie," May whispered. "Bye, Uncle Louis."

We heard their footsteps move away, and then it was silent.

I felt something square and hard poking into my leg.

May wiggled a little and moved it. "Sorry. That's my secret drawin' book. It used to be Bella's 'til she threw it away. I sneaked it out of the trash pile for my own.

"You probably wonder why I wanted a book. I wasn't schooled like Bella. So I can't write nor read. But I tell stories in my book with pictures instead."

Some quiet time passed. Then May began to whisper her freedom dreams as we lay there in the dark night. "Don't worry, Glory. We're goin' far up north where I'll be safe. And it'll be colder, so maybe you won't melt."

"And tell you something else. Someday, I'm gonna find my mama and daddy. Even though they were sold away when I was a baby, I know I'll find them."

CHAPTER 22
❧ Escape ❧
Glory's Story

The next morning, someone hitched horses to our wagon.

Giddyap!

The wagon lurched forward, and we left the plantation behind us.

May was quiet and still inside the crate so the driver wouldn't find out we had sneaked along for the ride. This crate had long, thin cracks, like the one I had come in from London. I could peek out enough to watch the sun rise.

We traveled all day. Now and then, May sipped water or nibbled the food Millie had given her.

That afternoon, the wagon stopped in a town. Our crate was unloaded. We were put in a stack of other boxes and packages. Upside down!

May gasped. "Oh, no. We can't stand on our heads all day. I'm gettin' dizzy."

"Can't you read?" we heard a man's voice yell. "That crate says OTHER END UP. Flip it around."

"Yes, sir," said another man. Our crate was quickly turned right side up.

"That's better," whispered May.

We stayed inside our crate for hours as voices and footsteps went past. What was going to happen? Did May know? She had to keep quiet, so she couldn't tell me.

Suddenly, someone rapped three times on our crate. May clutched me tightly.

"This box is mine," said a woman's voice. "Load it in my wagon, please."

Our crate was lifted into the back of another wagon. We traveled a few miles and then stopped. Someone got out of the wagon and came close to our crate.

"Are you all right in there?" asked the same woman's voice.

"Yes," whispered May.

"Only a few more miles," the woman promised.

Creak! The woman got in the front of the wagon again, and we started moving. A while later, we stopped. Someone pried open our crate's lid.

May popped out of the crate, under the star-filled sky. We had stopped in front of a stone house in a forest. "Is this the Undergound Railroad?"

A plump woman with freckles and light brown hair

smiled at her. "It sure is. We've been expecting you. How long have you been in this box?"

"A whole night and a day," said May. "So excuse me. I gotta go!"

May jumped from the wagon and ran behind a bush.

When she came back, the woman said, "Hurry into the house now. The Master of your plantation will be looking for you. He has probably offered a reward for your capture. So you'll have to hide out here until it's safe to travel."

"Yes, ma'am," said May.

"You were a brave girl to run away from the Cornelius Plantation by yourself."

"I wasn't alone." May pulled me out of the crate and showed me to the woman. "Glory was with me."

The woman laughed. "It's always best to travel with a friend."

She took us inside her house and cooked May a warm dinner. Later that night, she led us to a tiny room hidden behind a tall bookcase in the house. She pointed to a small bed. "This is where you'll sleep," she said.

May's eyes got big. "On the bed?"

The woman nodded. "Where else?"

"I've slept on the floor my whole life," said May.

"You're not a slave anymore," said the woman.

"But I'm not really free yet, am I?" asked May.

"Not until you get far enough north," the woman

told her. "You're still in Alabama. You have a long way to go before you reach safety."

After the woman left us, we lay on the soft bed. Just before she fell asleep, May whispered, "We did it, Glory. We escaped."

CHAPTER 23

❖ Adventures ❖

Glory's Story

So this was to be the journey by land that the puppet foretold, I thought. As he had predicted, adventures lay ahead.

Everywhere we went, there was always someone to guide us. They called themselves conductors on the Underground Railroad. We were passed from one conductor to another as we went farther and farther north toward freedom.

They led us through forests and fields. We hid in attics, stables, and even camped in the woods.

May always drew pictures of whatever happened to us in her black-and-gold-covered drawing book. She even drew a picture of us on the Underground Railroad, and a conductor showed her how to write our names on it. After she finished her drawings, she would lock the book with its tiny golden key.

One night, slave catchers chased us with bloodhounds.

"Into the stream. They can't track us there," our conductor told us.

We splashed through the stream for what seemed like miles. We crouched low as the dogs grew near. Then they ran right past us!

"They've lost our scent," said the conductor.

May was still breathing hard. "Did you hear, Glory? We're safe."

That night, the conductor took us to his home on the edge of a town. After supper, he watched May drawing a picture of him in her book. "You're a fine artist."

"I drew pictures of my slave days in this here book," May said proudly. "And now, I'm drawin' about our trip to freedom. I got pictures of all the conductors and places we stayed so I can always remember them."

The man looked through her book. "Your drawings are good. Maybe too good. If slave catchers saw them, they might recognize someone. Then they'd know who helped you to freedom. Helping slaves is against the law."

"I hadn't thought of that," said May. "You mean if I get caught with this book, you and the other conductors might go to jail?"

The man nodded.

All that night, May worried as we lay in bed in the hidden basement below the conductor's house. "If I get caught, I'll be punished," she whispered in the darkness.

"And so will the people who helped me. No tellin' what will happen to you, Glory."

In the middle of the night, she got up and lit a candle. She went around our room tapping on the floor and then the walls. Finally, she found some loose bricks in the wall and pulled them out. There was an empty space behind them.

"Perfect," I heard her whisper. Then she got back in bed. What was she planning?

The next morning, May asked the conductor, "Mister, does it get hot here?"

"Not this time of year," he said.

"But other times?" May went on. "Is it hot in the summer? In your basement?"

"It gets hot here, but the summers don't last as long as they do in the south. The basement is underground, so it stays cool year-round," he said.

We heard someone coming on horseback outside.

"Get your things together," the conductor told May. "Someone's here to take you to your next stop on the Underground Railroad."

May and I went down the small ladder to our basement room.

Carefully, she lay her drawing book inside the shadowy hiding place behind the bricks she had pulled out of the wall. She hugged me close until the man upstairs called to her to hurry.

"Comin'!" she called back to him.

I felt her tuck something under my hat. And then she gently set me behind the wall on top of her book.

"You won't melt here," she said. "And slave catchers won't get you."

She replaced the bricks one by one until I was hidden away.

"Watch over my secrets until it's safe to tell them," she whispered to me from outside the wall.

I will, I promised.

I heard the floorboards creak under her footsteps. And then she was gone.

I waited silently in my hiding place. I had a long wait ahead of me.

Over the following months, I heard other slaves who hid in the basement on their way to freedom. I heard talk of war and President Abraham Lincoln.

Years passed. Families came and went in the house. They stored things in the basement. They ate, slept, played, and gave parties in the house above me. They didn't even know I was there in the lonely basement. Waiting.

I stayed hidden for more than a hundred years, as the puppet had foretold.

Then, just a few weeks ago, I heard a crash. And loud voices. Men shouted at one another. More crashes.

Dust whooshed and the wall began to crumble. It was frightening!

Suddenly, the bricks in front of me were ripped away. Big hands in rough, dirty gloves pulled me from my hiding place.

"Ms. Tate! Come have a look at this!" the man holding me called.

A few minutes later, I was handed to a woman. She was brown like May. But I had a feeling she was living free. That's how I knew.

It was finally safe to tell May's secrets.

CHAPTER 24
❖ The Hiding Place ❖

"Let's look in Glory's hat. Maybe whatever May hid is still there," said Rose.

Rose, Lila, and Far Nana peered inside the hat.

Far Nana handed it to Lila. "Your finger is smaller than mine. Poke around and see if you find anything."

Lila poked. "I feel something," she said. She pulled a small piece of paper out of the hat's lining. It was folded into a tiny square. The old yellowish paper crackled as she unfolded it.

On one side of the paper, there was a drawing of a big girl and a small girl. They were standing on a railroad track under the ground. Crooked letters above the big girl spelled M-A-Y. Above the little girl, it said G-L-O-R-Y. There was also a drawing of a key with an arrow pointing to Glory.

"It's one of May's drawings!" said Lila.

"It's May and Glory on the Underground Railroad," said Rose. "The big girl is May, and the little one is supposed to be Glory!"

"But where is May's book? And her key?" Far Nana wondered aloud. "Why didn't Ms. Tate find them?"

Rose shook the hat. A tiny key fell out. Rose picked it up just as the doorbell rang.

Far Nana quickly filled out a Certificate of Wellness for Glory and rolled it up. Rose tied a ribbon around it.

Meanwhile, Lila rushed downstairs to see who their visitor was. "It's Ms. Tate!"

She flung the door open. "We found a key in Glory's hat," she blurted.

Ms. Tate stepped back. "What? Who's Glory?"

Far Nana and Rose hurried down the stairs to the front door. Far Nana invited Ms. Tate in and handed Glory and the certificate to her.

Ms. Tate smiled when she saw Glory. "How charming! I can hardly believe the change!"

Lila elbowed Far Nana. "Don't forget the other stuff."

Far Nana handed May's drawing and key to Ms. Tate. "We found these in the lining of your doll's hat."

Ms. Tate studied May's drawing. "What does it mean?"

"We think your house was a stop on the Underground Railroad!" said Lila.

Rose pointed at the drawing. "This is a girl and this is your doll. They are both on a railroad under the ground. See?"

"So the escaping slave girl is named May and my

doll is named Glory?" asked Ms. Tate. "And they traveled together on the Underground Railroad?"

"We believe so," said Far Nana.

"This is amazing!" said Ms. Tate. "I can't wait to tell my husband." She put a hand on the doorknob.

Then she turned back to Far Nana. "I almost forgot. I wanted to take some pictures of us with Glory, now that she's finished."

She flipped buttons on her camera to the right settings and gave it to Rose. "Do you mind?"

"Nuh-uh," said Rose. She took several photographs, trying to get the best angles.

While she was busy, the phone rang. Lila went to answer it. After Ms. Tate left, Rose found Lila on the phone in the living room.

"It's Mom," said Lila, holding the phone out toward Rose. "Dad was on at first, but he had to go help some Africa people. I talked already. Your turn."

Rose held the phone to her ear. "Hi, Mom."

"How's everything going at school?" her mom asked.

"Fine," said Rose. She told her the story about Nadia and Far Nana's underwear. Her mom laughed.

Lila overheard the story and began laughing, too. A minute later, Rose could hear her telling it to Far Nana in the other room.

Far Nana cracked up. "I wondered where my orange underwear went!"

The static cling underwear hadn't seemed so funny in class. But now it sort of did. Even to Rose.

Rose finished telling her mom everything else that had happened in the week since her parents had called last.

"Lila said you've had snow," said her mom. "That sounds good. Africa's seasons are the opposite of yours, so it's summer here now. It's roasting hot. Sometimes I feel like I'm melting."

"Good thing you're not made of wax," said Rose.

"What?" her mother asked.

"Never mind," said Rose. "It's a long story."

CHAPTER 25
❧ News ❧

One morning a week later, Rose shook Lila awake. "Get up. Remember our plan?"

Lila blinked at her, trying to wake up. "Oh, yeah. Let's go!" She hopped out of bed and followed Rose down the hall.

They knocked on Far Nana's bedroom door.

"Come in," she called in a sleepy voice.

Rose and Lila opened the door. Far Nana was in bed, reading the morning newspaper.

"Up and Adam!" Rose and Lila shouted. "Yay! We said it first!"

They smacked hands together in victory.

"Who's Adam?" asked Far Nana.

"I don't know. It's what you say every morning," said Lila.

Far Nana laughed. "I say 'up and at 'em'. That's an expression that means get up and get after them. 'Them' being people, work, fun, life."

"Oh," said Rose and Lila.

Rose turned her head sideways to read the paper Far Nana was holding. "Hey! There's a story about Glory in the newspaper!"

Far Nana flipped the newspaper around so she could see what Rose was talking about. She read the headline and part of the story aloud:

CIVIL WAR DOLL HOLDS KEY TO DIARY OF A RUNAWAY SLAVE

The drawing diary of a runaway child slave named May and her doll, Glory, has been found in the basement of Alex and Andrea Tate's house. The Tate home was a stop on the Underground Railroad and has been named an historic landmark. The diary and doll will soon be on display at the Oak Hill Museum.

"Sounds like Ms. Tate found May's diary in the basement wall after all," said Far Nana.

"Now Glory's famous. And she got to tell May's story to everyone," said Rose.

"Look! You're in the paper, too, Far Nana! It's a picture Rose took of you, Ms. Tate, and Glory," said Lila.

Far Nana smiled at the photograph. "Well, for Pete's sake."

Rose and Lila looked at each other and then back at Far Nana.

"Who's Pete?"

Glossary

antique doll   a doll made long ago

big house   nickname for a slave owner's house on a plantation

bisque   porcelain that is not very shiny

china   shiny porcelain

doll auction   a public sale of dolls in which an auction-eer shows dolls to a group of people who can bid money for them

kiln   a special oven used for baking ceramic and porce-lain at very hot temperatures

master   a plantation owner who had slaves

plantation   a very big farm in the southern United States

porcelain   a fine-grained ceramic material that is heated in a kiln and is breakable

slave   a person forced to allow another person to own them

slave auction   a public sale of slaves, when slavery was legal. Prices paid for a slave were usually between $250 and $1,500. In the United States (and most other places in the world), it is now illegal to own or sell a person.

Underground Railroad   a network of paths and hiding places in the United States and Canada leading slaves to areas where they could be free

Questions and Answers About
Slavery and the Underground Railroad

How did slavery begin in America?
Africans were first brought to America as slaves in 1619. More slaves arrived during the next 190 years.

Slavetraders kidnapped them from their homes and often separated them from their families. The Africans had to cross the Atlantic Ocean from Africa to America on crowded ships. Men, women, and children were chained together and given little food or water on the voyage. They were scared, angry, and sad. Many became sick or died.

Once they arrived in America, the Africans were forced into slavery. They were made to do a lot of work they didn't want to do for no pay.

Many Americans thought slavery was wrong. In 1808, a law was passed making it illegal to bring more slaves into the United States. However, slaves that were already in the United States were not yet set free.

What jobs did slaves do on a plantation in the South?
Field slaves plowed, planted, and harvested the crops. It

was very hard work. They worked from sunrise to sunset, six days a week. They hardly ever got to rest. Sometimes, they were whipped if they did not work fast enough.

House slaves did many jobs at the big house. They spun wool, sewed and mended clothing, cleaned, cooked, and took care of the Master's children and livestock.

Slaves had to do any chore their Master told them to do, or else they might be punished or sold.

Did slave children have to work?
Slave children did simple jobs when they were young. They gathered eggs, fed chickens, carried water, swept the floors, and weeded gardens.

When they had time, slave children played games with one another or with the Master's children. They enjoyed games like I Spy, hide-and-seek, horseshoe toss, and marbles. Girls sometimes drew a dollhouse in the dirt and played in it with their dolls.

But between age eight to twelve, friendships between slave children and the Master's children often ended. At this age, slave children began to work as hard as their parents in the Master's fields or home. The Master's children went on to learn skills that would help them run the plantation someday.

Did slaves do anything besides work?
Slaves tried to remember Africa and their ancestors by

singing African songs and doing African dances. It was against the law for a slave to learn to read or write. So they told stories about Africa to their children.

On Sundays, some slaves held secret church services in nearby fields, barns, or in their homes. They were not allowed to have unsupervised meetings.

What was the Underground Railroad?

The Underground Railroad was not a real railroad. It did not have trains or tracks. It was a network of paths, hiding places, and people that led slaves to freedom. The secret paths helped slaves escape from the southern United States where slavery was allowed, to free states in the North, or to Canada.

Between 35,000 and 100,000 slaves may have escaped on the Underground Railroad. No one knows the actual number because it wasn't safe to keep records. Runaway slaves and those who helped them escape were harshly punished if they were caught.

A former slave named Harriet Tubman helped many slaves escape on the Underground Railroad. A reward was offered for her capture, but she was never caught.

Why did some people want to keep slavery in the United States?

Slaves were not paid for the work they did on southern plantations. Plantation owners knew that if slavery ended, they would have to pay their workers. That would make it more expensive to grow cotton, sugarcane, tobacco, corn, and rice on their plantations. So they wanted slavery to continue.

Northern states didn't have plantations. Factories and businesses in the North made a profit even though they paid their workers. They did not need slaves and thought slavery was wrong. They wanted slavery to end.

What ended slavery in the United States?
In April 1861, the Civil War began. There were many reasons for the war. One of the most important reasons was that northern states and southern states couldn't agree about slavery.

Northern states formed an army. So did the southern states. The two armies fought bloody battles.

On January 1, 1863, President Abraham Lincoln issued the Emancipation Proclamation. This ordered the southern states to free their slaves. There were still about four million slaves in the United States. Most of them were in the South. Many plantation owners ignored President Lincoln's order. The fighting continued.

Southern General Robert E. Lee finally surrendered to Northern General Ulysses S. Grant on April 9, 1865. The Civil War was over.

The thirteenth amendment, which made slavery illegal, was added to the U.S. Constitution in December 1865.

How did the lives of former slaves change after the Civil War?

After the Civil War, former slaves had to be paid for their work. Some of them stayed to work on plantations as paid employees. Others left to find family members who had been sold away. Still others found work in cities.

Former slaves could go to school to learn to read and write after the war. They could legally marry. They could own their own farms and livestock, or start their own businesses.

Most important was the fact that no one owned them anymore. No one could buy or sell them. They were free to make choices and decisions for themselves.

Watch for the fourth book in the
✚ Doll Hospital ✚ series,

Charlotte's Choice:
THE STORY OF A SHAKER VILLAGE,
coming soon.

"Eenie, meanie, miney, moe," said Rose.

It was Saturday morning. She and her little sister, Lila, lay on their bedroom floor. They studied the Oak Hill Amusement Park map spread out between them.

"There are too many good rides. I don't know which one to go on first," said Rose.

"I do." Lila pointed to a ride that looked like a spinning purple spider. "I'm going on the Screaming Purple Swirly." She looked at the park map more closely. "Or maybe the Fire-breathing Roller Coaster."

"See? I told you it was hard to choose," said Rose. "You can't do both first."

"Why not?" asked Lila. She was trying to drive Rose crazy.

Rose leaned toward Lila and gave her The Eye. "I've decided which ride I want to do first. I'm going on the Screaming Purple Little Sister Stomper. Right now!"

Lila laughed and scooted away before Rose could pounce. "Why don't you go on the Fire-breathing Rosertoaster instead?"

"Shhh! Listen." Rose held up a hand for Lila to be quiet. They heard the click-clack sound of their grandmother's beaded necklaces out in the hall. "Here comes Far Nana."

"Do you think she'll take us?" asked Lila.

Rose answered Lila in a voice loud enough for their grandmother to hear in the hall. "Sure, why not? Far Nana is sooo nice. Of course she'll take us."

Far Nana smiled at them from the doorway. The yellow smiley-face button pinned on her dress smiled at them, too. "Go where?"

"Oh, hi, Far Nana," Rose said. She pretended like she hadn't heard her grandmother coming from a mile away. "We have a great idea for our first day of spring vacation. You're going to lo-o-o-ve it."

"We want to go to Oak Hill Amusement Park," said Lila. "Look!"

Rose and Lila jumped up to show Far Nana the map.

"This does look like fun," began Far Nana.

"Yay!" said Lila.

"But I already made plans to take you girls to Mulberry Shaker Village," said Far Nana.

Lila slumped over. "Not yay."

"Where?" Rose asked in disbelief.

Far Nana looked from Rose to Lila and back. Her smile faded, and she began twisting her beaded necklaces. "Mulberry Shaker Village."

"Like salt shakers? A whole village of them?" asked Lila.

"No. The Shakers were people who lived together like a big family. They built the village more than two hundred years ago. Now tourists can visit it to see how the Shakers once lived."

"But we could go there anytime," said Rose.

Far Nana shook her head no. "An old friend of mine who works there called and invited us to the village. She asked me to repair a Shaker doll while we visit."

Far Nana knew all about dolls. She had a doll hospital in her house. She was a doctor, just like Rose and Lila's parents. Only Far Nana fixed dolls and their parents fixed people.

"What about Oak Hill Amusement Park?" asked Rose.

"We can go another time," said Far Nana.

"No we can't. This week is a once-in-a-springtime event especially for spring vacation. It says so right here."

Lila held the park map closer to Far Nana's sparkly gator-green glasses to be sure she could read the big purple letters. They said:

Come to Oak Hill Amusement Park's
Once-in-a-Springtime Event!
Special Rides and Activities for Kids on Spring Vacation

"I wish you'd said something sooner," said Far Nana.

"Why didn't you say something sooner about the Shaker place?" asked Lila.

"I wanted it to be a surprise," explained Far Nana.

"It is," said Rose. "The crummy kind."

"We told the other kids at school we were going to the amusement park," said Lila. "We can't be the only ones who don't show up!"

"I'm sorry, but I just spoke to my friend on the phone," said Far Nana. "I promised her we'd be at the village by tonight."

Rose tried to think of reasons they couldn't go. She came up with one. "Mom and Dad won't know where to call us."

"And what about the cats?" asked Lila.

"I'm going to give your parents the village's phone number so they can call you there," said Far Nana. "And I'm going to ask your friend Nadia from next door to feed the cats and play with them while we're gone."

"But—" said Rose.

Far Nana folded her arms like she meant business. "I've made my decision. I think you'll have a good time on this trip if you give it a chance. Now let's get packing. It's a three-hour drive." She turned and left their bedroom.

Rose flopped on the bed. "No-Fair-Far-Nana. That's her new name."

"When I grow up, I'm going to let my granddaughters do whatever they want on spring vacation," said Lila. "But we have to do what she tells us to. Mom and Dad said."

"Mom and Dad!" said Rose. "Great idea. Let's call them. Maybe they can change Far Nana's mind."

"It costs a lot to call Africa. I thought we were only supposed to call them for emergencies," said Lila.

"This is an emergency," said Rose. "Let's go."

While Far Nana was in her room packing, the girls tiptoed downstairs. They dialed their mom and dad's phone number in Africa.

Rose and Lila held the phone between them, so they could both hear. They listened to their mom's voice on the answering machine. "You've reached Doctors Elton and Elton. Please leave a message."

As usual, they had to leave voice mail. Their parents were always busy working in the African villages.

Rose's words tumbled out fast. "Mom, Far Nana is being mean."

"She's making us go to the salt shaker village for spring vacation," Lila butted in.

"But we want to go to Oak Hill Amusement Park," said Rose. "Make her stop bossing us around, okay?"

"Yeah. She's ruining our vacation," said Lila.

They were quiet for a second, listening to long-distance air.

Rose wound her fingers in the curls of the phone cord. "I wish you would come home. I miss you."

"Yeah," said Lila. "Ditto."

Joan Holub

About the Author

When Joan Holub was a girl, her best friend, Ann, lived right down the street. Ann had lots of toys. But she had one special doll that Joan loved best — a beautiful ballerina. It had lace-up shoes and a frilly satin tutu. Its body was jointed and bendable.

After a few years, Joan's family moved away. Ann gave the doll to Joan as a going-away present. Joan named the doll Annie, after her friend. She made lots of clothes for Annie, using her mother's sewing machine.

Joan played with Annie so much that she wore her out. Annie's arms and legs came apart. She needed help! So Joan and her mother took Annie to a doll hospital. There, Annie's arms and legs were put back together. She even got a new wig.

Annie and some of her doll friends live in Washington State with Joan, her husband, George, and their two cats.

Joan Holub is the author and/or illustrator of many books for children. You can find out more about Joan and her books on her Web site, *www.joanholub.com.*

✦ Doll Hospital ✦

Love and care...
and stories to share.

Tatiana

Goldie

Collect them all—
one free paper doll in each book.

Download free clothing for all of your paper dolls,
and find out more about Doll Hospital:
www.scholastic.com/titles/dollhospital

Available wherever you buy books, or use this order form.